Different Paths To The Waterfall

Elliot Kent

Published by Michael Pollick, 2024.

This is a work of fiction. Similarities to real people, places, or events are entirely coincidental.

DIFFERENT PATHS TO THE WATERFALL

First edition. August 22, 2024.

Copyright © 2024 Elliot Kent.

ISBN: 979-8227564917

Written by Elliot Kent.

Table of Contents

Different Paths To The Waterfall

Elliot Kent

From The Modern Beatitudes, Suggested By Pope Francis

Silent Warriors

In the quiet corners of the heart, where shadows linger and whispers of betrayal echo, there lies a strength, unyielding, like ancient roots gripping the earth. Blessed are those who walk the narrow path, who bear the weight of injustice, the heavy cloak of sorrow draped upon their shoulders, yet still rise with the dawn, eyes turned toward the light. They are the silent warriors, the unsung heroes, who endure the slings and arrows of malice, the barbs of envy, and the poison of deceit.

With every wound, they gather fragments of their shattered spirit, weaving them into a tapestry of resilience. They know the taste of bitterness, the sting of betrayal, yet they choose to soften their hearts, to cradle the very souls that sought to harm them. Forgiveness blooms in the cracks of their pain, a fragile flower pushing through the rubble, reaching for the sun. It is not weakness but a fierce, defiant grace, a refusal to be defined by the darkness that surrounds them.

They whisper prayers into the void, not for vengeance, but for understanding, for the brokenness that drives others to inflict harm. They see the humanity in the eyes of their oppressors, the wounds that fester beneath the surface, and they choose compassion over contempt. In their hearts, they carry the weight of the world, yet they refuse to let it crush them. Instead, they transform it into a balm, a healing salve for their own wounds and those of others.

Blessed are those who remain faithful, who hold onto hope like a flickering candle in the storm, illuminating the path for others lost in darkness. They walk with grace, embodying the truth that love, even in its most challenging forms, is the greatest act of rebellion against the evils inflicted upon them.

https://app.videogen.io/view/dgcsex

Seeing Humanity

Blessed are those who dare to look,
not just glance, but truly see,
the eyes of the abandoned,
those deep wells of unspoken stories,
where hope flickers like a candle,
fighting against the wind,
the storm of indifference,
the weight of neglect.
In those eyes, a universe unfolds,
a tapestry woven with threads of despair,
yet threaded through with resilience,
the quiet strength of survival,
the echo of laughter lost,
the shadow of dreams deferred.
Blessed are those who bend low,
who kneel in the dust,
who offer their hands,
not as saviors, but as companions,
who understand that closeness is a bridge,
not a chasm,
that to hold space is to hold hearts,
to listen is to love,

to share silence is to share breath.
In the gaze of the marginalized,
there lies a mirror,
reflecting our own fears,
our own fragility,
and in that reflection,
we find the courage to connect,
to reach across the divide,
to dismantle the walls built by fear,
to recognize the sacred in the ordinary,
the divine in the discarded.
Blessed are those who see the beauty,
the raw, unfiltered beauty,
in the faces of those society forgets,
who understand that every scar tells a story,
every tear is a testament,
and every smile,
a revolution.
They are the ones who ignite the spark,
who fan the flames of compassion,
who remind us that we are all threads,
woven together in this vast, chaotic tapestry,
and that to look into the eyes of the abandoned
is to look into the eyes of our shared humanity.
https://app.videogen.io/view/dlvsqg

Guardians of Tomorrow

In the quiet dawn, where the sun spills gold upon the earth, I find
solace in the whispers of the trees, their leaves a gentle chorus, singing
of resilience. Blessed are those who tread softly upon this sacred ground,
who cradle the soil in their hands, who understand that every blade of
grass is a testament to life, a promise of tomorrow.

They rise with the sun, these guardians of our common home, their hearts beating in rhythm with the pulse of the planet. They listen to the rivers, flowing with stories of old, carrying the weight of memories, each drop a reminder of the delicate balance we must uphold. They plant seeds of hope in the cracks of concrete, nurturing dreams that sprout against all odds, defying the shadows of neglect.

Blessed are those who see beauty in the mundane, who find poetry in the rustling of leaves, the laughter of children playing in the park, the embrace of a warm breeze. They understand that every creature, from the smallest ant to the soaring eagle, plays a role in this intricate tapestry of existence. They stand as sentinels, protecting the fragile threads that bind us to one another, to the earth, to the sky.

In their hands, they hold the power to heal, to mend the wounds inflicted by greed and indifference. They speak for the voiceless, the rivers choked with plastic, the forests silenced by chainsaws. They are the dreamers, the doers, the ones who dare to envision a world where harmony reigns, where the air is pure, and the waters flow clear.

Blessed are those who protect and care, for they are the architects of a future where love for our common home flourishes, where every heartbeat resonates with the promise of a better tomorrow.

https://app.videogen.io/view/weuqeo

Blessed Sacrifice

In the quiet corners of the heart, where shadows dance with light, there lies a truth, unadorned and raw, that whispers softly to the weary soul. Blessed are those who step beyond the familiar embrace of their own comfort, who trade the warmth of their own hearth for the chill of another's despair. They are the ones who see the world not as a collection of faces, but as a tapestry woven with threads of struggle and hope, each strand a story, each knot a lesson.

They rise before dawn, not for the promise of a new day, but for the call of the forgotten. They walk the streets where laughter has faded, where the echoes of joy are drowned by the weight of sorrow. In their eyes, the flicker of compassion ignites a fire that warms the coldest nights, a beacon for those lost in the fog of despair. They know the taste of sacrifice, the bitter sweetness of giving without the expectation of return, and yet, they find richness in the act itself.

Blessed are those who renounce the easy path, who choose to bear the burdens of others as if they were their own. They understand that comfort is a fleeting illusion, a soft pillow that lulls the spirit into complacency. Instead, they embrace the jagged edges of reality, the rawness of life unfiltered, and in that embrace, they find a profound connection to the human experience.

They are the unsung heroes, the quiet warriors of kindness, whose hearts beat in rhythm with the pulse of the world. In their renunciation, they discover a deeper joy, a fulfillment that transcends the self. Blessed are they, for in their sacrifice, they illuminate the path for others, turning the darkness into a canvas of light, a testament to the power of love in action. https://app.videogen.io/view/gpfwab

Tapestry of Hope

In the quiet corners of our hearts, where faith flickers like a candle, we gather, hands clasped, voices raised, weaving a tapestry of hope. Blessed are those who pray, who bend their knees in the stillness of dawn, whispering dreams of unity into the vastness of the universe. Each prayer a thread, each word a stitch, binding us in a fabric of love that transcends the boundaries we've built.

We are the seekers, the wanderers, yearning for a table where all are welcomed, where the bread is broken and shared, where the cup overflows with grace. In the echoes of ancient hymns, we find our rhythm, a melody that dances between denominations, a harmony that sings of our shared humanity. Blessed are those who work, who toil in the fields of compassion, sowing seeds of understanding in the soil of diversity, nurturing the fragile blooms of fellowship.

Let us rise, not as strangers, but as kin, united in our quest for a communion that knows no walls. In the laughter of children, in the tears of the broken, we see the face of Christ reflected back at us, urging us to embrace the beauty of our differences, to celebrate the colors of our faiths. Blessed are those who dare to dream of a world where love reigns, where the sacred and the secular intertwine, where every voice is heard, every story honored.

Together, we forge a path, a journey toward a horizon painted with the hues of hope, where the sun rises on a new dawn of understanding. Blessed are those who pray and work, for they are the architects of a future where communion is not just a word, but a living testament to the power of love, a promise that we are all, in our essence, one.

https://app.videogen.io/view/odwsrz

Divine Reflections

In the quiet corners of the heart, where shadows dance and light flickers, there lies a truth, a whisper of divinity woven into the fabric of existence. Blessed are those who see God in every person, who peer beyond the surface, past the masks we wear, and glimpse the sacred spark that resides within. They walk among us, these seekers, with eyes that shimmer like stars, illuminating the mundane with the glow of the eternal.

They understand that every soul is a universe, a tapestry of dreams and struggles, laughter and tears, woven together by the threads of humanity. They see the divine in the weary traveler, the child with dirt-streaked cheeks, the elderly man with stories etched in the lines of his face. They recognize the sacred in the mundane, the holy in the ordinary, and in doing so, they invite us to join them on this pilgrimage of discovery.

To strive to make others also discover Him is a calling, a gentle nudge towards awakening. It is the soft touch of a hand on a shoulder, the shared smile that bridges the chasm of isolation, the words of kindness that echo in the silence. It is the art of seeing, of acknowledging the divine dance in every encounter, of nurturing the seeds of love that lie dormant in the hearts of those we meet.

In a world that often forgets, they remind us that we are all reflections of the same light, fragments of a greater whole. They teach us that to love is to see, to embrace the sacred in our shared humanity. Blessed are those who walk this path, for they are the architects of hope, the bearers of grace, the ones who illuminate the way for others to find the God that resides within.

https://app.videogen.io/view/ynaakp

From The Seven Pillars Of Islam

Divine Oneness

In the stillness of dawn, when the world holds its breath, I feel the pulse of the universe, a singular heartbeat echoing through the vastness of existence. One. Just one. The essence, the breath, the whisper that threads through every atom, binding the stars to the soil beneath my feet. In this oneness, I find the tapestry of life, woven with threads of light and shadow, joy and sorrow, each strand a testament to the divine unity that cradles us all.

I walk through the chaos of the day, where voices clash and hearts divide, yet beneath the cacophony, there lies a profound truth, a silent song that sings of connection. Every face I meet, every soul I encounter, reflects a fragment of that singular light. We are not separate; we are notes in a symphony, each contributing to the harmony of existence. The mountains, the rivers, the very air I breathe—all are manifestations of that one essence, a reminder that we are part of something greater, something eternal.

In moments of doubt, when shadows loom large, I close my eyes and remember: there is no other, only the One. The One who knows my heart, who sees my struggles, who embraces my imperfections. In surrendering to this truth, I find peace, a sanctuary amidst the storm. I am not alone; I am cradled in the arms of the infinite, a drop in the ocean of divinity.

And so, I rise, each day a new chance to honor that oneness, to reflect it in my actions, to love fiercely and without reservation. For in loving,

I acknowledge the divine spark in every being, and in that acknowledgment, I become a vessel of unity, a bridge across the divides, a testament to the beauty of the One.
https://app.videogen.io/view/apbulm

Wings of Faith

In the quiet corners of my heart, I feel their wings,
silent messengers, woven from the fabric of light,
they glide through the unseen,
their presence a gentle whisper,
a reminder of the divine,
each one a thread in the tapestry of faith,
each one a guardian, a guide,
watching, waiting,
their eyes like stars,
illuminating the shadows of doubt.
They are the breath of creation,
the pulse of the universe,
carrying the weight of prayers,
lifting them to the heavens,
where the words dissolve into the ether,
and the heart finds solace,
in the knowledge that I am never alone,
that they dance around me,
in moments of joy, in moments of despair,
their laughter mingling with my tears,
their strength fortifying my fragile spirit.
I think of Gabriel,
the angel of revelation,
who brought forth the words,

the sacred verses that echo through time,
like a river flowing,
nourishing the roots of my belief,
and I wonder,
what it must be like to hold such power,
to be the bridge between the divine and the mortal,
to carry the weight of truth on feathered shoulders.
And there are others,
the scribes of fate,
etching my story in the book of life,
each moment a stroke of ink,
each breath a testament to the journey,
reminding me that every heartbeat is a gift,
every trial a lesson,
and in the stillness of the night,
I close my eyes,
and feel their presence,
a chorus of faith,
singing the song of existence,
reminding me,
I am cradled in the arms of the unseen.
https://app.videogen.io/view/mywwho

Sacred Whispers

In the quiet of dawn, when the world holds its breath,
I find solace in the whispers of ancient pages,
the ink still fresh, the words alive,
each letter a thread woven into the fabric of my soul.
The revelations, a cascade of divine wisdom,
flowing from the heart of the Eternal,
guiding the lost, the weary, the seekers of truth.
In the Torah, the stories of creation unfold,

the covenant, a promise etched in the stars,
the laws, a compass for the wandering heart,
reminding us of our sacred duty,
to love, to serve, to remember the One.
The Psalms sing of hope, of despair,
the cries of the human spirit,
echoing through valleys and mountains,
a reminder that in our struggles,
we are never alone,
for the Divine listens,
the Divine understands.
The Gospel, a testament of love,
the light that breaks through the darkness,
the parables, a mirror reflecting our own journeys,
inviting us to embrace compassion,
to walk the path of humility,
to find grace in our imperfections.
And then, the Qur'an, the final revelation,
a symphony of guidance,
each verse a drop of rain on parched earth,
nourishing the seeds of faith,
reminding us of our purpose,
to submit, to strive, to seek justice,
to be the stewards of this fragile world.
In every book, a heartbeat,
in every word, a connection,
the threads of belief intertwining,
binding us to the Divine,
to each other,
to the sacred journey of existence.
In the revelations, I find my anchor,
my compass, my song,

a testament to the power of faith,
the beauty of belief,
the promise of the unseen.
https://app.videogen.io/view/kzwpyx

Legacy of Prophets

In the quiet corners of my heart, I cradle the whispers of the Prophets,
each one a thread woven into the tapestry of faith,
a lineage of light stretching across the ages,
from Adam, the first breath of humanity,
to Muhammad, the final echo of divine guidance.
They walked among us,
flesh and spirit intertwined,
messengers of a truth that transcends time,
each voice a beacon,
each story a lesson carved in the stone of existence.
Moses, with his staff, parting the seas of despair,
a leader forged in the fires of struggle,
carrying the weight of a people,
the commandments etched in the heart of a nation.
Jesus, a whisper of love,
healing the broken,
turning water into wine,
a testament to the miracles that dwell in the mundane,
reminding us that divinity often wears the guise of humanity.
And there's Noah,
building hope in the face of ridicule,
his ark a sanctuary for the weary,
a promise that even in the storm,
faith can weather the fiercest winds.
Each Prophet, a chapter in the sacred book of existence,
their lives a mirror reflecting our own struggles,

our own aspirations,
reminding us that we are not alone,
that the divine speaks through the hearts of those chosen.
In this belief, I find my anchor,
a connection to the unseen,
a reminder that the path is illuminated by their footsteps,
that faith is not a solitary journey,
but a collective pilgrimage,
where every prayer, every act of kindness,
is a tribute to the legacy they left behind,
a call to embody their teachings,
to carry the torch of truth,
and to believe, always, in the power of the Prophets.
https://app.videogen.io/view/xmahih

Reflections of Judgment

In the quiet corners of my mind, I gather the whispers of the ancients, the echoes of a truth that trembles beneath the surface of everyday life. The Day of Judgment, they say, a reckoning, a moment suspended in time where the scales of justice hang heavy, waiting for the weight of our deeds. I envision a vast expanse, a horizon stretching beyond comprehension, where the sun bows low and shadows stretch long, where every soul stands bare, stripped of pretense, of the masks we wear in the light of day.

What will I carry? The laughter shared, the tears shed, the moments of kindness that flickered like stars in the dark? Or will it be the silence of indifference, the choices made in haste, the words left unspoken, the hands that turned away? Each heartbeat a reminder, each breath a chance to realign, to seek the light in the labyrinth of existence.

I ponder the weight of intention, the purity of thought, how the heart can be a compass, guiding us through the fog of our own making. The Day of Judgment is not just a distant promise; it is a mirror reflecting the essence of our being, a call to accountability that resonates in the depths of our souls.

Will I stand proud, or will shame cloak me like a shroud? The scales tip, the ledger unfolds, and in that moment, the truth of my life will be laid bare, unvarnished, raw. I am both the architect and the witness of my fate, crafting a narrative with every choice, every act of love or neglect.

In the end, it is not the fear of judgment that stirs my heart, but the hope that I may rise, transformed, into the light of mercy, embraced by the grace that awaits beyond the horizon.

https://app.videogen.io/view/wvcfof

Threads of Destiny

In the tapestry of existence, threads woven with intention,
the fabric of fate stretches, a delicate balance,
between the choices we cradle in our palms
and the unseen hands that guide us,
the whisper of destiny, a soft echo in the chambers of our hearts.
What is premeasurement, if not the dance of the universe,
where every star is a promise, every breath a decree,
the ink of the cosmos spills stories before we arrive,
each moment a brushstroke on the canvas of time?
I stand at the crossroads of my desires,
the weight of my dreams heavy upon my shoulders,
yet, in the quiet corners of my mind,
I hear the gentle reminder,
that I am but a traveler,
navigating the rivers of possibility,
my will a vessel, yet the current flows unseen,
carving paths I cannot foresee.
In the heart of uncertainty, I find solace,
for in the embrace of Qadar,
there lies a profound freedom,

the surrender to the rhythm of the divine,
the understanding that every joy, every sorrow,
is a note in the symphony of my existence,
composed before I took my first breath.
I am both the seeker and the sought,
the architect of my choices,
yet the blueprint was drawn long before my hands could shape it.
In this paradox, I find my strength,
to trust in the unseen,
to dance with the shadows of fate,
to believe that every twist and turn,
every tear and triumph,
is a step towards the greater tapestry,
where my story intertwines with the infinite,
and in that, I find my peace,
my faith, my unwavering belief in the premeasured grace of life.
https://app.videogen.io/view/jygqrp

Eternal Whispers

In the quiet of the night, when shadows stretch long and the world holds its breath, I ponder the weight of existence, the fragile thread that binds us to this earthly realm. Life, a fleeting whisper, a flicker in the vastness of time, yet it pulses with the promise of something beyond, something eternal.

Belief in resurrection, a seed planted deep within the heart, nourished by faith and the echoes of ancient truths. It speaks of a day when the dust of our bodies will rise, when the very essence of who we are will awaken from the slumber of the grave. Each heartbeat, a reminder of the divine, each breath, a testament to the journey we undertake, a pilgrimage through the trials of this world, leading us to the gates of the next.

What is death, but a doorway, a passage into the unknown? A transformation, a shedding of the skin that binds us, a release from the chains of time. In the stillness, I can almost hear the call, the gentle beckoning of souls long departed, waiting for the moment when the trumpet will sound, and the earth will tremble with the weight of resurrection.

In that moment, all will be revealed, the tapestry of our lives unfurling before us, threads of joy and sorrow woven together in a divine design. We will stand, bare and unmasked, before the Creator, our deeds laid out like stars in the night sky, illuminating the path we chose.

And in that reckoning, the heart will know its truth, the spirit will soar, liberated from the confines of flesh, embraced by the light of eternity. So I hold this belief close, a lantern in the dark, guiding me through the labyrinth of life, whispering of hope, of renewal, of the promise that we are never truly lost.

https://app.videogen.io/view/ntbfyo

From The Teachings Of Confucius

Hidden Beauty

Everything has beauty, but not everyone sees it.
It's in the cracks of the pavement, the way the sun spills through the leaves,
the laughter of children echoing in the alleyways,
the old man feeding pigeons, his hands trembling like autumn leaves.
Beauty is the soft hum of a city waking up,
the rhythm of footsteps on wet sidewalks,
the way a stranger's smile can light up a dreary day,
if only for a moment.
But not everyone sees it.
Some are too busy, too burdened by their own shadows,
lost in the chaos of their thoughts,
the weight of their worries,
the noise drowning out the whispers of wonder.
They walk past the wildflowers growing through the cracks,
the vibrant colors splashed against the gray,
and they don't notice,
they don't stop,
they don't breathe in the scent of possibility.
And yet, beauty is there,
in the mundane, the overlooked, the ordinary.
It's in the way the rain dances on rooftops,
the way the moon hangs low, a silver coin in a velvet sky,

the stories etched in the lines of a face,
the warmth of a hand held in silence.
It's the fleeting moments,
the glances exchanged between strangers,
the shared laughter over spilled coffee,
the comfort of a familiar song on a lonely night.
Beauty is everywhere,
waiting to be discovered,
like a hidden treasure beneath layers of dust.
But not everyone sees it.
Some choose to look away,
to focus on the flaws, the imperfections,
the chaos that drowns out the light.
Yet, for those who dare to pause,
to open their eyes,
to truly see,
the world is a canvas,
painted with hues of hope,
a reminder that beauty exists,
even in the most unexpected places.
https://app.videogen.io/view/ksuybo

Embracing Change

In the quiet corners of my mind, I ponder the weight of constancy, the allure of steadfastness. They must often change, those who seek happiness, those who chase wisdom like a flickering flame, elusive yet intoxicating. I think of the trees, their leaves dancing in the wind, shedding the old to embrace the new, a cycle of rebirth, a testament to resilience.

What is it to be constant? To cling to the familiar, the comfortable, the known? Yet, in that grip, do we not suffocate the spirit? Happiness, that capricious muse, flits from one heart to another, a butterfly in a garden of shifting seasons. I've learned that to hold on too tightly is to invite despair, to anchor oneself in the past while the present beckons with open arms.

Wisdom, too, is a fickle companion. It whispers in the ears of those willing to listen, but it demands change, a shedding of old skins, a willingness to be reborn. Each lesson learned is a thread woven into the fabric of our being, but to grow, we must unravel, we must question, we must dare to step into the unknown.

I see the faces of those who resist, who fear the tides of change, their eyes clouded with the weight of what was. They cling to their certainties, their routines, but in doing so, they miss the symphony of life that plays just beyond their grasp.

So I choose to embrace the flux, to dance with the chaos, to welcome the storms that shape me. For in the act of changing, I find my truth, my joy, my wisdom. The only constant is the willingness to evolve, to let go, to become.

https://app.videogen.io/view/ukgjjm

Inner Strength

What the superior man seeks is in himself,
a quiet strength, a reservoir of purpose,
a mirror reflecting the depths of his own soul,
he digs deep, unearthing the roots of his desires,
not in the fleeting shadows of others,
but in the solid ground of his own convictions.
He walks a path carved by his own hands,
each step a testament to the battles fought within,
the whispers of doubt silenced by the roar of belief,
he knows that the treasure lies not in the accolades,
not in the fleeting applause of a crowd,
but in the stillness of self-discovery,
where the heart beats in rhythm with the universe,

and the mind dances with the stars,
he seeks wisdom in the silence,
truth in the chaos of his thoughts,
and finds that the greatest journey is inward,
the greatest conquest is the one of self.
What the small man seeks is in others,
his gaze fixed on the reflections around him,
he gathers scraps of validation,
like a child collecting shiny stones,
searching for worth in the eyes of the world,
he measures his success by the applause of strangers,
his happiness a fragile thread woven from their opinions,
he chases shadows,
believing that fulfillment lies in the embrace of the crowd,
but the crowd is fickle,
and the applause fades like echoes in an empty hall,
he finds himself lost,
adrift in a sea of borrowed dreams,
never knowing the power of his own voice,
never realizing that the light he seeks
has always been waiting,
quietly flickering within,
a flame yearning to be kindled,
if only he would turn inward,
if only he would dare to seek.
https://app.videogen.io/view/hcciel

The Dance of Time

In the quiet corners of my mind, I hear the whisper of a truth, a gentle
reminder that the journey is not a race, but a dance, a slow waltz through
the corridors of time. Each step, no matter how hesitant, carries weight,
carries purpose. It does not matter how slowly you go, I tell myself, as I

navigate the winding paths of uncertainty. The world rushes by, a blur of faces and voices, all clamoring for urgency, for the quick fix, the instant gratification. But here I am, taking my time, savoring the moments that others overlook, the small victories that bloom like wildflowers in the cracks of concrete.

I think of the tortoise, steadfast and unwavering, while the hare sprints ahead, blinded by ambition, only to falter in the end. It is not the speed that defines success, but the resolve to keep moving, to keep believing, even when the road stretches long and the horizon seems distant. Each breath I take is a testament to my persistence, a reminder that progress is progress, no matter how minuscule.

With every stumble, I learn, I grow, and I rise again, dusting off the remnants of doubt that cling to my spirit. I embrace the slow, the deliberate, the beautiful unfolding of my own story. The clock may tick relentlessly, but I am not bound by its tyranny. I carve my own path, one step at a time, weaving through the tapestry of my existence, and in that, I find freedom.

So let them rush, let them chase the fleeting shadows of time. I will walk my own pace, for in the end, it is not the speed that matters, but the journey itself, the unwavering commitment to keep moving forward, to never stop.

https://app.videogen.io/view/zdasvx

Courage to Act

To see what is right, and not to do it,
is to stand at the edge of a precipice,
the wind howling, whispering truths,
the ground beneath trembling with potential,
and yet, we hesitate,
frozen in the grip of indecision,
clutching our fears like talismans,
as if they could shield us from the weight of choice.

What is courage, if not the trembling heart
that dares to leap,
to embrace the unknown with open arms,
to shatter the silence of complacency
with the thunder of action?
And what of principle,
that steadfast compass guiding us through the fog,
the moral anchor that keeps us grounded
when the tides of doubt threaten to sweep us away?
To see what is right is a gift,
a flash of clarity in a world muddied by gray,
but to act upon it,
to transform vision into reality,
requires a fire that burns within,
a willingness to risk, to sacrifice,
to stand alone if necessary,
to face the scorn of those who cling to the shadows,
who whisper that it's easier to conform,
to follow the path of least resistance.
Yet, in that moment of choice,
when the heart races and the mind spins,
we must ask ourselves,
what is the cost of silence?
What is the price of inaction?
For every moment we turn away,
we chip away at our own integrity,
we dull the brilliance of our own spirit,
and we become mere spectators
in a world that cries out for change.
So let us not falter,
let us not shrink back,
for to see what is right,

and to do it,
is to reclaim our courage,
to honor our principles,
to step boldly into the light.
https://app.videogen.io/view/nbtydq

The Cost of Revenge

Before you embark on a journey of revenge, dig two graves, they say, but what do they know of the heart's wild terrain? The ache that festers, the fire that ignites when betrayal seeps into your veins, a poison that twists your thoughts into a labyrinth of shadows. Revenge is a siren's call, sweet and seductive, promising solace in the echo of retribution. But listen closely, for the path is strewn with thorns, each step a reminder of the cost, the toll it takes on the soul.

You think you'll find justice, but what is justice but a fleeting ghost, a mirage that dances just beyond your reach? You envision their downfall, the satisfaction of watching them crumble, but in that moment of triumph, you'll find yourself standing alone, the weight of their ruin heavy on your shoulders. You dig one grave for them, yes, but the second grave is for the part of you that once believed in forgiveness, in healing, in the possibility of moving on.

Revenge is a mirror, reflecting back the darkest corners of your own heart. It whispers sweet nothings, lulling you into a false sense of empowerment, but the truth is, it chains you to the past, shackles your spirit in a cycle of pain. You become the architect of your own despair, building a monument to bitterness that towers over your life.

So before you take that first step, before you let the fire consume you, consider the graves you'll dig. One for them, yes, but the other for the dreams you once held, the love you once knew, the peace that now feels like a distant memory. In the end, revenge is a thief, stealing not just from them, but from you, leaving behind only ashes and echoes of what could have been.

https://app.videogen.io/view/mrxufo

Embrace of Silence

Silence, the quiet companion,
the one who sits beside me,
unwavering, unjudging,
in the cacophony of the world,
where voices clash like swords,
and words spill like ink,
tainting the air with their weight.
In the stillness, I find solace,
a refuge from the chaos,
where thoughts can breathe,
untethered, unfettered,
drifting like leaves in an autumn breeze.
Silence wraps around me,
a soft blanket,
whispering secrets only I can hear,
the truths that tremble in the shadows,
the fears that linger just out of sight.
It holds my hand when the storm rages,
when the world demands my voice,
and I am too weary to speak.
In its embrace, I am safe,
no need for masks, no need for pretense,
just the raw pulse of existence,
the heartbeat of the universe,
echoing in the quiet corners of my mind.
Silence does not betray;
it does not twist my words,
does not turn my heart against itself.
It listens,

a patient ear to my unvoiced dreams,
the hopes that flutter like moths,
the regrets that cling like cobwebs.
In the absence of sound,
I find clarity,
the kind that shimmers like dew at dawn,
the kind that cuts through the fog,
revealing the path I must tread.
Silence is the friend who knows,
who understands without needing to pry,
who stands guard over my secrets,
a sentinel in the night,
reminding me that in the quiet,
I can hear my own heart,
and that, perhaps,
is the loudest truth of all.
https://app.videogen.io/view/euihcx

Inspired By Jewish Holidays

Sacred Togetherness (Shabbat)

In the hush of twilight, the world exhales,
and the sun dips low, painting the sky in hues of gold and lavender,
a gentle reminder that time, like a river, flows,
and here, in this sacred pause, we gather,
we breathe, we become.
Candles flicker to life,
their flames dance, weaving stories of ancestors,
each wick a bridge to the past,
illuminating the faces of those we love,
their laughter echoing through the walls of our hearts.
With each flicker, a prayer rises,
a whisper of gratitude for the week that was,
for the burdens lifted, the joys embraced,
the mundane transformed into the miraculous.
The challah, braided like our lives,
soft, warm, kissed by the hands of time,
breaks easily, a symbol of abundance,
sharing, as we pass it round the table,
the sweetness of honey, the bitterness of life,
all intertwined,
reminding us that in every crumb,
there is a blessing,
in every moment, a chance to reconnect.

We sing, voices weaving together,
melodies that float like doves,
carrying our hopes, our dreams,
our fears, laid bare in this sacred space.
The laughter of children, the sighs of the weary,
all harmonizing in the symphony of Shabbat,
where time stands still,
and the world beyond fades,
leaving only this moment,
this sanctuary of peace.
As the stars blanket the sky,
we nestle into the warmth of togetherness,
the chaos of life paused,
and in this stillness,
we find ourselves,
woven into the fabric of the universe,
held in the embrace of the divine,
a reminder that we are never alone,
that rest is holy,
that love is everlasting.
https://app.videogen.io/view/sewtgh

Moonlit Beginnings (Rosh Chodesh)

In the hush of twilight, the moon, a silver coin, flips through the sky, marking the birth of a new month, Rosh Chodesh, a whisper of beginnings, a soft sigh of renewal. The calendar, a tapestry of time, unfurls before us, each thread a story, each day a chance to weave our lives anew. The women gather, their laughter a melody, a sacred song rising like incense, filling the air with warmth, with hope, with the promise of what's to come.

In the flickering candlelight, we stand, hands clasped, eyes closed, hearts open. We breathe in the sweetness of the month to come, the fruit ripening in the orchards of our dreams. We speak the names of those we love, weaving them into our prayers, a tapestry of remembrance and aspiration. Each name a thread, each prayer a stitch, binding us together, connecting the past to the present, the present to the future.

The moon, a witness to our secrets, our joys, our sorrows, hangs low, cradling our wishes in its luminous embrace. We dance in circles, our feet brushing against the earth, our spirits soaring, lifting us beyond the mundane, beyond the ordinary. There is power in this gathering, in this celebration of femininity, of strength, of resilience. We are the keepers of the flame, the nurturers of life, the voices that echo through generations. As the moon waxes, so do our hopes, our dreams, our aspirations. We cast away the shadows, the doubts that linger like ghosts in the corners of our minds. Rosh Chodesh, a sacred moment, a breath of fresh air, a reminder that with each new month, we are given the gift of possibility, the chance to start anew, to embrace the light that beckons us forward.

https://app.videogen.io/view/npjypc

Twilight Reflections (Rosh Hashanah)

In the hush of twilight, the air thick with the scent of apples, honey drips like memories, sweet and sticky, clinging to the edges of time. A new year unfurls before us, a blank scroll, waiting for the ink of our intentions, our hopes, our whispered prayers. The shofar's call pierces the silence, a ram's horn echoing the heartbeat of a people, awakening the dormant seeds of possibility buried deep within our souls.

We gather, hands clasped, eyes lifted, hearts open wide, as if to catch the blessings that rain down like golden leaves in the autumn breeze. Each note of the shofar a reminder, a summons to reflect, to return to the essence of who we are, to the stories woven into the fabric of our existence. We are the echoes of ancestors, their laughter mingling with our tears, their struggles etched in the lines of our palms.

As we dip the apple, we taste the promise of sweetness, a covenant renewed, a pledge to strive for kindness, to seek forgiveness, to embrace the light even when shadows loom large. The past lingers, a delicate thread, binding us to the lessons learned, the mistakes made, the love shared. We stand on the precipice of change, the horizon painted with the colors of hope, each sunrise a reminder that we are not alone in this journey.

With every breath, we inhale the possibility of transformation, exhale the burdens that weigh heavy on our shoulders. This is our moment, a sacred pause in the relentless march of time. As the stars begin to twinkle, we whisper our dreams into the universe, trusting that they will find their way back to us, like the sweet taste of honey on our tongues, a promise of what is yet to come.

https://app.videogen.io/view/nudaje

Dawn of Reflection (Tzom Gedalia)

In the stillness of the dawn, a hush falls over the world, a sacred pause, as the sun hesitates on the horizon, casting shadows long and weary, tracing the outlines of memories etched deep in the heart. Tzom Gedalia, a day of reflection, a day of mourning, where the echoes of loss ripple through the fabric of our being, reminding us of the fragile threads that bind us to one another, to our past, to the stories that linger like whispers in the wind.

We gather, not in celebration, but in solemnity, our hearts heavy with the weight of history, the weight of lives lost, the weight of choices made and paths not taken. The air is thick with the scent of remembrance, of prayers woven into the tapestry of time, each word a stitch, each silence a pause, as we confront the shadows of our ancestors, those who walked before us, who faced their own trials, their own tribulations.

In the depths of our sorrow, we find a flicker of hope, a glimmer of resilience, as we honor the fallen, the ones whose dreams were cut short, whose voices were silenced, yet whose spirits linger, urging us to remember, to reflect, to rise above the ashes of despair. We fast, not just to empty our bodies, but to fill our souls, to create space for the lessons of grief, for the wisdom that emerges from the cracks of our brokenness. As the day unfolds, we confront our own fragility, our own vulnerabilities, and in that confrontation, we find strength. We are not alone; we are threads in a vast tapestry, woven together by love, by loss, by the indomitable spirit that refuses to fade, that insists on lighting the way forward, even in the darkest of times. Tzom Gedalia, a reminder that from mourning can spring new life, new beginnings, if only we dare to embrace the journey.

https://app.videogen.io/view/rgbtei

Reflections of Renewal (Yom Kippur)

In the quiet of the evening, as the sun dips low,
I find myself wrapped in a shroud of reflection,
the weight of a year's choices heavy on my heart,
each moment a pebble in my pocket,
some smooth, others jagged,
each a reminder of paths taken, words spoken,
and the silence that followed.
I walk through the corridors of memory,
the echoes of laughter mingling with tears,
the faces of loved ones,
some still here, others just shadows,
fading like the light of day.
Yom Kippur, a day of atonement,
a sacred pause,
the world holds its breath,
the air thick with unspoken regrets,
and the hope for forgiveness,
like a fragile bird, wings trembling,
ready to take flight.
I close my eyes and listen,

to the whispers of ancestors,
to the prayers that rise like incense,
each word a thread, weaving us together,
a tapestry of faith and longing.
The fast stretches on,
a physical emptiness,
but within, a feast of introspection,
a banquet of the soul,
where I confront the shadows,
the parts of me I'd rather hide,
the anger, the pride, the moments I turned away.
I seek the light,
in the cracks of my imperfections,
the beauty of vulnerability,
the strength in vulnerability,
and in the stillness, I find clarity,
the promise of renewal,
the chance to begin again.
As the sun sets,
I lift my gaze,
ready to embrace the unknown,
to step into tomorrow,
with a heart open wide,
and a spirit unburdened,
for this is the gift of Yom Kippur,
the chance to write a new story,
with every breath, a prayer,
for healing, for love, for peace.
https://app.videogen.io/view/sauddl

Autumn Embrace (Sukkot)

In the embrace of autumn's breath, I find myself beneath the fragile canopy of leaves, a temporary dwelling, a sukkah, a reminder of journeys past, of wandering through deserts, of faith wrapped in the warmth of harvest. The branches above, a patchwork of green and gold, whisper stories of resilience, of the fragile balance between shelter and exposure, a dance between the known and the unknown.

Here, I gather with family, our laughter mingling with the rustling of the wind, the echoes of prayers rising like smoke from the candles we light, flickering against the night's encroaching chill. We share fruits of our labor, the bounty of the earth laid before us, each bite a testament to survival, to gratitude, to the sweetness of life. The pomegranates burst with ruby seeds, a symbol of abundance, each one a promise, a blessing, a memory of what it means to be rooted yet free.

In this moment, I am reminded of the fragility of existence, how the walls we build are often illusions, how the sky above, vast and open, invites us to look beyond. I think of those who have wandered, who have sought refuge beneath stars that have witnessed their tears and triumphs. I think of the stories we carry, woven into the fabric of our being, each thread a connection to the past, to the ancestors who stood in similar spaces, their hopes echoing through time.

As we sit together, the world outside fades, and I am enveloped in the warmth of tradition, of community, of love. Sukkot teaches me to embrace the fleeting, to find joy in impermanence, to celebrate the harvest of my heart, the abundance of togetherness, the sacredness of this moment, this life, this journey.

https://app.videogen.io/view/esoles

Celestial Traditions (Shemini Atzeret and Simchat Torah)

In the stillness of the night, the sky wraps around us, a velvet cloak of stars, each one a witness to the stories we carry, the burdens we bear. Shemini Atzeret, a pause, a breath held tight, the world exhaling in gratitude, and I stand here, heart open, arms raised to the heavens, feeling the weight of tradition, the echo of prayers whispered across generations. In the flickering candlelight, I sense the presence of those who came before me, their laughter mingling with the rustle of the Torah scroll, its parchment soft and worn, a testament to our journey, to the struggles and triumphs etched in every letter, every word. Simchat Torah, the joy of the scroll, the dance of the faithful, twirling under the moonlight, spinning with the rhythm of our history, a celebration of endings and beginnings, a cycle unbroken, a promise renewed.

We gather, hearts intertwined, voices rising like incense, a symphony of gratitude for the gift of the law, for the stories that bind us, that teach us resilience in the face of despair, hope in the shadow of doubt. Each verse, a thread in the tapestry of our lives, woven with love and loss, joy and sorrow, a reminder that we are never alone, that our faith carries us forward, even when the path is shrouded in darkness.

Tonight, I hold the Torah close, its weight grounding me, its wisdom lifting me, a bridge between the past and the future. I dance, not just for myself, but for every soul that has walked this earth, for every tear shed, every triumph celebrated. In this moment, I am part of something greater, a lineage of light, a testament to survival, to joy, to the unyielding spirit of my people, forever turning the scroll, forever embracing the dance of life.

https://app.videogen.io/view/qlsjuw

From The Sufi Poet Rumi

Tightrope of Life

Life is a balance, a tightrope strung between the weight of memories and the lightness of release. We cling to moments like children grasping at balloons, bright and buoyant, yet tethered to the ground by the fear of losing them. Each laugh, each tear, each heartbeat echoes in the chambers of our minds, reminders of what was, what is, and what could be. We hold on, knuckles white, to the past, believing that in the grasp of nostalgia lies safety, that in the familiar, we find ourselves.

But then there's the whisper of change, soft yet insistent, urging us to let go, to open our hands and watch those balloons drift into the sky. Letting go is a lesson in trust, a leap into the unknown, where the air is thin and the ground is distant. It asks us to believe that new colors await us, new laughter, new tears, new heartbeats. It's a dance, a rhythm of release, a surrender to the flow of time that carries us forward, that nudges us gently from the comfort of the past.

Yet, in this delicate balance, we learn that holding on isn't inherently wrong. It's the warmth of love, the roots of identity, the threads that weave our stories. But to grow, to breathe, to embrace the full spectrum of existence, we must also learn the art of letting go. It is not a severing, but a transformation, a metamorphosis where we learn to cherish the echoes while making space for the symphony yet to come.

So we walk this tightrope, heart in hand, a dance of opposites, where every step is a choice, every breath a reminder that life is both the anchor and the wind, the memory and the promise, the holding on and the letting go.

https://app.videogen.io/view/zlxcqe

Wounds and Light

The wound is the place where the Light enters you, they say, but what of the darkness that surrounds it? What of the shadows that dance in the corners of your heart, whispering secrets of pain and regret? It's in those moments, when the world feels heavy, when the weight of unspoken words presses down like a leaden shroud, that the wound becomes a chasm, a gaping hole where hope once thrived. Light, they say, enters through the wound, but does it not also bleed out, like a river running dry, leaving behind only echoes of laughter and the ghost of what once was?

I remember the first time I felt the sting, the sharp bite of betrayal, the sweet poison of love turned sour. It carved a path through my soul, a jagged line that opened me up to the universe, raw and exposed. In that moment, I was both shattered and whole, a paradox wrapped in skin. The Light, it seeped in like dawn breaking through the darkest night, illuminating the corners I had long forgotten. It showed me the beauty in the cracks, the way the scars tell stories, the way they shimmer under the right angle, catching the sun just so.

But still, I wonder, what of the wounds that never heal? The ones that fester and pulse with the weight of unacknowledged grief? They too hold a light, a flicker of resilience, a reminder that survival is an art. It is in the vulnerability of our wounds that we find connection, that we learn to embrace the light and the dark, the joy and the sorrow, the beautiful mess of being alive. So yes, the wound is the place where the Light enters you, but it is also where you learn to dance with your shadows, to embrace the whole of your existence.

https://app.videogen.io/view/pplwkx

Born to Soar

You were born with wings,
an intricate tapestry of dreams woven into your very essence,
yet here you are,
clinging to the ground,
like a fragile leaf caught in autumn's chill,
wondering if the sky is just a distant memory,
a whisper of what could be,
while you shuffle through the dust of yesterday.
Why prefer to crawl through life?
Is it the weight of expectations,
the heavy cloak of fear draped across your shoulders,
the echo of voices telling you to stay small,
to fit neatly into the boxes they've crafted,
to be the good child, the obedient worker,
the one who never stirs the waters,
never challenges the winds?
But deep within,
the fire flickers,
a restless spirit yearning to break free,
to spread those wings,
to taste the wind and dance with the clouds.
Imagine the colors you could paint across the sky,
the stories you could weave in the air,
the laughter that could bubble up,
unfettered and wild,
if only you would dare to rise,
to leave behind the safety of the ground,
to embrace the chaos of flight,
to trust the currents that promise to lift you higher.
You were born with wings,
not to be tucked away,

not to be hidden beneath the weight of doubt,
but to soar, to explore,
to discover the vastness of your own heart,
the uncharted territories of your spirit.
So tell me,
what is it that holds you back?
What anchors you to this earth,
when the sky calls your name,
and the horizon beckons with the promise of freedom?
Unfurl those wings,
let them catch the light,
and remember,
you were never meant to crawl.
https://app.videogen.io/view/kpyuov

Echoes of the Mountain

The world is a mountain,
its peaks rising high, sharp against the sky,
each word you utter, a stone cast into the void,
bouncing back, reverberating through the canyons of your mind.
What you say, how you say it,
the echoes return,
a chorus of your own making,
and you stand there,
listening to the sound of your own voice,
wondering if it's the truth or just a reflection,
the mountain holds your secrets,
your fears, your hopes,
and the whispers of your heart,
climbing higher,
the air thins,
and still, you shout into the abyss,

"Do you hear me?"
The mountain knows,
it knows the weight of your words,
the power they carry,
how they can uplift or crush,
how they can build bridges or walls,
and as you listen,
the echoes twist and turn,
becoming something new,
a tapestry woven from the threads of your thoughts,
each repetition a reminder,
a lesson learned,
a chance to change the story,
to reshape the narrative that spirals back to you,
the world is a mountain,
solid, unyielding,
yet within its granite heart,
there's a softness, a vulnerability,
a place where your voice can find refuge,
where your words can dance,
where they can soar,
and when you finally silence the noise,
the echoes fade,
leaving you with a stillness,
a clarity,
and in that moment,
you realize,
the mountain is not just a reflection,
it's a conversation,
a dialogue between you and the universe,
and every word you speak
is a step towards understanding,

a path carved into the stone,
leading you home.
https://app.videogen.io/view/rgsgvw

Embracing Change

Be like a tree, they say,
and let the dead leaves drop,
but what if I'm afraid of the bare branches,
the starkness of winter's grip,
the vulnerability of standing still,
naked against the cold winds of change?
I cling to the remnants of what was,
the vibrant hues of summer,
the laughter that danced in the sunlight,
the memories that rustle like leaves,
crunching underfoot,
each step a reminder of what I've lost.
Yet, there's a wisdom in the shedding,
a quiet strength in the letting go,
the way the tree knows it must,
to breathe, to grow,
to make room for the new,
the soft buds of spring that promise life,
the green that will unfurl,
if only I could trust in the cycle,
the rhythm of seasons,
the inevitability of change.
But here I stand,
gripping the past like a child holding tight to a favorite toy,
afraid to release it,
afraid to let it fall,
to crumble into the earth,

to become nourishment for something greater.
What if I could be like the tree,
rooted yet flexible,
standing tall in the storm,
allowing the winds to strip me bare,
to expose my core,
to let the rain wash away the remnants of yesterday?
To be like a tree,
to embrace the cycle,
to let go of what no longer serves me,
to trust in the promise of tomorrow,
to find beauty in the emptiness,
to know that in every drop,
there is a chance to rise anew,
to reach for the sky,
to dance once more in the sunlight,
unencumbered, unfettered,
a testament to resilience,
a celebration of life.
https://app.videogen.io/view/axmcvw

Whispers of Growth

In the quiet of dawn, when the world is still wrapped in a blanket of soft whispers, I find solace in the gentle rhythm of my thoughts. Raise your words, not your voice, they say, and I wonder, what does it mean to speak softly yet profoundly? The thunder may roar, but it is the rain that nurtures the earth, coaxing life from the soil, coaxing flowers to bloom in vibrant defiance of the storm.

In this cacophony of existence, we often mistake volume for power, believing that the loudest shouts will shatter the silence, will command attention. Yet, I've seen the quiet strength of a single raindrop, how it caresses the petals of a flower, how it seeps into the ground, weaving stories of growth beneath the surface. It does not demand; it simply is.

What if we chose to be like the rain? To let our words fall softly, each one a delicate promise, each syllable a seed planted in the hearts of others? I think of the conversations that linger long after the last word has been spoken, the ones that resonate like echoes in the chambers of memory, the ones that build bridges instead of walls.

In the end, it is not the thunderous applause that marks our impact, but the quiet moments of connection, the gentle nudges of understanding that spark change. To raise our words is to embrace vulnerability, to speak truth with tenderness, to cultivate a garden of thoughts that flourish in the minds of those around us.

So let us be rain, let us be the nurturing force that encourages growth, that whispers encouragement into the chaos. Let us remember that it is not the volume of our voices but the depth of our words that truly makes the flowers bloom.

https://app.videogen.io/view/yivzew

Cosmic Dance

What you seek is seeking you, a dance of shadows and light, a whisper in the wind that carries the echoes of your heart. You chase dreams like fireflies, darting through the night, believing they're just out of reach, but what if they're closer than you think? What if every longing, every desire, is a mirror reflecting your own essence, a call from the universe, a gentle nudge reminding you that you are not alone in this quest?

You stand at the edge of the world, searching for answers in the vastness of the sky, but the truth lies not in the stars above, but within the depths of your soul. The love you crave, the peace you yearn for, they're not distant shores, but seeds planted in the fertile soil of your being, waiting for the right moment to bloom.

Every step you take, every breath you draw, pulls you closer to the very thing you seek. It's a magnetic pull, an invisible thread weaving through time and space, binding you to your desires, drawing them nearer, like moths to a flame.

So why do you hesitate? Why do you doubt? The universe is alive with possibility, a tapestry of connections waiting to be unraveled. Embrace the uncertainty, let go of the fear that holds you captive, for what you seek is not just a destination, but a journey, a transformation.

In the quiet moments, listen to the heartbeat of your dreams, feel the rhythm of their pursuit echoing in your chest. They are not lost; they are waiting for you to recognize that you are the seeker and the sought, intertwined in this beautiful cosmic dance. Trust in the process, for what you seek is seeking you, always, relentlessly, with open arms.

https://app.videogen.io/view/srffuq

Embrace Your Magnitude

In the quiet corners of your mind, where doubts whisper like shadows, you must remember—stop acting so small. You are not merely a flicker in the vast night, a fleeting thought lost in the cacophony of existence. No, you are the universe in ecstatic motion, a symphony of stars colliding and dancing, a tapestry woven from the threads of cosmic wonder. Feel the pulse of galaxies within you, the rhythm of creation that thrums in your veins, each heartbeat echoing the birth of worlds.

Why do you shrink back, constricting your brilliance like a flower folding its petals in the face of dawn? You are the light that ignites the darkness, the spark that ignites the fire, the laughter that shatters silence. Embrace your magnitude; let it swell within you, a tidal wave of possibility crashing against the shores of convention. You are the storm, the calm, the wild wind that howls through the canyons of despair, reminding the world of its own grandeur.

Imagine the weight of the cosmos resting on your shoulders, not as a burden but as a crown, a testament to your existence. You are the echoes of ancient stars, the dreams of countless lives, the hopes that shimmer in the spaces between breaths. Each moment is a canvas, and you—oh, you—are the artist, splashing colors of passion and purpose, crafting a masterpiece out of chaos.

So, rise. Lift your chin to the sky and let your spirit soar. Stop acting so small. You are not confined to the narrow definitions of what it means to be human. You are the universe, ever-expanding, ever-evolving, a dance of creation that knows no bounds. Let your essence explode into the world, a brilliant supernova of potential, for you are alive, and that is the greatest miracle of all.

https://app.videogen.io/view/iumbrw

From The Meditations of Marcus Aurelius

Morning Mantra

When you arise in the morning, let the light spill through your window like a whispered secret, a gentle reminder that today is a gift, unwrapped and waiting. Think of the air, crisp and alive, filling your lungs with the promise of possibility. Each breath, a declaration of existence, a dance of molecules that brings you closer to this moment, this heartbeat, this chance to be.

Consider the miracle of thought, the way your mind weaves dreams and plans, a tapestry of hopes stretching into the horizon. Every idea, a spark igniting the canvas of your day. In this vast universe, your consciousness is a rare jewel, a flicker of awareness amidst the infinite. Cherish it, for it is the lens through which you experience the world, the brush with which you paint your reality.

And oh, the joy of enjoyment! The simple pleasures that beckon like old friends. The warmth of sunlight on your skin, the taste of morning coffee, rich and bold, awakening your senses. Laughter that bubbles up like a brook, spilling over into the spaces between thoughts. These moments, fleeting yet profound, are the threads that weave the fabric of your life.

Then there is love, the most precious of all. The way it wraps around you, a comforting embrace, binding you to others in a shared journey. The laughter, the tears, the quiet understanding that passes between souls. Love is the heartbeat of existence, a reminder that you are never truly alone.

So as you rise, let gratitude fill your heart, a soft echo of the privilege it is to be alive. To breathe, to think, to enjoy, to love—this is your morning mantra, a celebration of the miracle of being. Embrace it, hold it close, and let it guide you through the day.

https://app.videogen.io/view/booidc

Embrace Life

It is not death, no, not the quiet end that steals away breath and light, but the unmarked days, the hollow echoes of a life unlived, that should send shivers down the spine. To wake each morning, to feel the sun kiss your skin, and yet to remain shackled by the weight of "what ifs" and "could have beens." A man should fear the silent surrender to the mundane, the slow fade into a life of routine where dreams gather dust, where hope is a distant whisper drowned by the noise of conformity.

What is life without the spark of adventure, the thrill of the unknown? To stand on the precipice of possibility and turn back, to let fear dictate the rhythm of your heart, to let the clock tick away moments that could have been filled with laughter, with love, with the raw, unfiltered joy of existence. Isn't it the missed opportunities that haunt the soul, the paths not taken that linger like shadows?

Imagine the stories left untold, the songs unsung, the colors never painted on the canvas of your days. A life half-lived is a tragedy, a book with pages torn out, a melody played in silence. The true death lies not in the final breath but in the moments we let slip through our fingers, in the dreams we bury beneath the weight of fear and doubt.

So, rise up! Embrace the chaos, the uncertainty, the exhilarating mess of living. Dance in the rain, chase the stars, speak your truth, and let your heart beat wildly against the confines of what is safe. For it is not death that we must fear, but the fading away of our spirit, the surrender to a life never fully embraced. Live, oh live, and let each heartbeat be a testament to the beauty of existence.

https://app.videogen.io/view/zkwzgj

Resilience Unveiled

In the quiet chambers of my mind, where shadows dance with the flicker of doubt, I stand before the mirror, a mosaic of scars and stories etched upon my skin. Each mark, a testament to battles fought, to wounds that whispered their tales of betrayal and loss. I could cradle them, nurture their pain like a mother does a child, but what if, just what if, I chose to reject the very essence of injury?

What if I peeled back the layers, stripped away the weight of memory, and let the air kiss the rawness of my existence? I am not the sum of my hurts; I am the breath that rises with the dawn, the heartbeat that thrums with possibility. I refuse to let the echoes of past injuries define my present. I am not the shattered glass that reflects a distorted image; I am the light that refracts, creating rainbows from fragments.

In the stillness, I hear the whispers of resilience, urging me to rise, to dance on the edge of my own narrative. The injury itself, that specter looming large, begins to dissolve, like mist under the sun's embrace. I am not a victim; I am a warrior, adorned in the armor of my choices, fierce in my rejection of despair.

With each breath, I reclaim my story, weaving threads of strength through the fabric of my being. The pain, once a heavy cloak, now drapes lightly, a reminder that I have lived, that I have loved, that I have survived. I stand tall, unyielding, casting aside the shadows that once clung to my spirit. I am the architect of my healing, the master of my fate, and in this moment, I declare: injury is but a fleeting illusion, and I, I am free.

https://app.videogen.io/view/puagqa

Acceptance and Love

Acceptance is a gentle whisper in the chaos of life, a soft nudge that reminds me to breathe, to let go of the frayed edges of what I cannot change. Fate, that invisible thread weaving through the tapestry of existence, binds me to moments I never chose but must now embrace. It's in the laughter shared over coffee on rainy days, the warmth of a hand held tightly when the world feels cold, the quiet understanding that blooms in silence. I learn to accept these things, not as burdens but as gifts wrapped in the mundane, the extraordinary hidden in the ordinary. Love, oh love, it's the wild dance of souls colliding, unexpected and fierce. It's the way a friend's smile can light up the darkest corners of my heart, how a stranger's kindness can restore my faith in humanity. Fate brings us together, a cosmic arrangement, and I find myself grateful for every encounter, for every fleeting moment that etches itself into my being. I commit to loving these people with all my heart, to pouring my essence into every shared experience, to being fully present, to listening deeply, to laughing until my sides ache.

Yet, there's a bittersweetness in this acceptance, a recognition that not all bonds last, that some will drift away like leaves carried by the wind. But even in the letting go, I hold onto the love, the lessons learned, the memories that linger like echoes in a vast canyon. I embrace the beauty of impermanence, the fragility of connection, and I vow to love fiercely, to accept wholeheartedly, to dance with fate's whims and cherish the people who color my world. Because in the end, it's all intertwined, a beautiful mess of acceptance and love, binding us together in this fleeting, precious life.

https://app.videogen.io/view/zhnuej

Embrace the Divergence

What does it mean to stand apart, to dance on the edges of a crowd that swells and thrums with the pulse of conformity? The object of life, they say, is not to find comfort in numbers, not to blend into the tapestry of the majority, but to navigate the labyrinth of self, to carve a path through the thicket of expectation and emerge whole, unscathed, unshackled. Insanity whispers sweet nothings, luring us into its embrace, promising safety in surrender, warmth in the fold of collective madness. But what of the soul that yearns for clarity, for the sharpness of truth that cuts through the fog of sameness? I watch as faces blur, as thoughts become echoes, as dreams are swallowed whole by the insatiable maw of the ordinary.

To escape the ranks of the insane is to embrace the chaos within, to acknowledge the wildness that thrums beneath the surface. It is the courage to stand in the quiet, to listen to the heartbeat of the universe, to find solace in solitude. In a world that clamors for allegiance, I seek the sanctuary of my own mind, where ideas bloom like wildflowers, untamed and free.

Here, I find the beauty of divergence, the strength in vulnerability, the power of being unafraid to question, to challenge, to disrupt the status quo. I am not a cog in the machine, nor a shadow in the parade. I am a seeker, a wanderer, a voice that dares to rise above the din.

So let them march, let them chant their hollow slogans, let them revel in their shared delusions. I will carve my own path, one step at a time, until I find the resonance of my truest self, a beacon shining defiantly against the tide of the insane.

https://app.videogen.io/view/absncy

Soul Palette

In the quiet chambers of my mind, I wander through the hues of my thoughts, vibrant and muted, swirling like paint on a canvas, each stroke a reflection of what I choose to dwell upon. It is a kaleidoscope of emotions, a spectrum where joy dances with sorrow, where hope mingles with despair. I realize now, the soul, that intricate tapestry woven from the threads of my musings, becomes a mirror to the colors I allow to seep into my being.

What shades do I cherish? The golden warmth of laughter, the deep blues of longing, the fiery reds of passion? Or do I let the grays of doubt, the blacks of fear, seep in, tinting my spirit with shadows? I stand at the crossroads, a painter with an empty palette, the brush in my hand trembling with the weight of choice. Each thought a pigment, each worry a stain, and I must decide which colors will define me.

I think of the moments when my heart swells with gratitude, the soft greens of contentment blooming within, how they illuminate the darkest corners of my existence. I think of the times I have wallowed in regret, the murky browns that cling like mud, weighing me down, dragging my soul into the depths of despair. I ponder the power of intention, the act of choosing thoughts that uplift, that inspire, that transform.

And so, I commit to this journey of self-creation, to paint my soul with the brilliance of possibility, to embrace the vibrant, the alive, the dynamic spectrum of existence. I understand now: my thoughts are the brush, my soul the canvas, and with each conscious choice, I am the artist, the creator of my own vivid reality.

https://app.videogen.io/view/spzfrt

From The Teachings of Gautam Buddha

New Beginnings

Every morning, the sun spills its golden warmth across the world, a silent reminder that we are reborn, fresh from the dreams that wove through our minds like threads of possibility. The weight of yesterday's burdens, those shadows that clung to us, dissolve with the dawn. Each day is a blank canvas, untouched, waiting for the strokes of our choices, our intentions, our actions.

What did I do yesterday? A question that lingers like a fog, but today, today is an invitation. It whispers in my ear, urging me to shed the past like an old skin, to rise from the ashes of yesterday's mistakes and breathe in the crisp air of potential. Today is a gift, a fleeting moment in the vast expanse of time, and what I do with it matters most.

I can choose to be kind, to extend a hand to someone who stumbles, to share a smile that ignites warmth in another's heart. I can choose to create, to let my thoughts spill onto the page, to paint my world with the colors of my imagination. I can choose to forgive, to release the grip of grudges that weigh down my spirit like anchors in a stormy sea.

Today, I can be brave, stepping into the unknown with a heart wide open, ready to embrace whatever comes my way. The past is a ghost, a mere echo of who I was, and it cannot tether me. Today is alive, pulsing with the energy of new beginnings, and I am the architect of this moment.

Every morning, we are born again, and what we do today, oh, it matters most. It is the heartbeat of our existence, the rhythm of our lives, a chance to dance in the light of possibility. So here I stand, ready to write my story anew.

https://app.videogen.io/view/nnwtpq

The Weight of Anger

Anger, a tempest brewing in the depths of my chest, a fire that flickers and roars, demanding to be felt, to be unleashed. It whispers, "Let me out, let me out," as if it holds the key to liberation, as if it can cut through the chains of restraint. But oh, the irony, the cruel twist of fate, for in that very release, I find my own shackles tightening around my spirit.

You will not be punished for your anger, they say, but in truth, it is the anger that punishes. It wraps its fingers around my throat, squeezing, squeezing until I can hardly breathe. It colors my thoughts, distorts my vision, turning the world into a battleground, where every slight feels like a dagger, every word a weapon. I lash out, I scream, I rage, but in the aftermath, I am left hollow, a shell of who I was, haunted by the echoes of my fury.

And in the quiet moments, when the storm subsides, I see the wreckage left in its wake—the friendships frayed, the love turned cold, the laughter silenced. I am not a warrior; I am a casualty of my own making, a prisoner in a cell of my own design. I thought anger would be my shield, my sword, but it has become my prison, the bars forged from resentment, the walls painted with regret.

So I stand here, grappling with the truth that anger is not a release; it is a thief. It steals my joy, my peace, my ability to connect. In its fierce embrace, I find myself lost, wandering through the shadows of what could have been, yearning for the light of understanding, for the balm of compassion, for the quiet strength that comes from letting go.

https://app.videogen.io/view/ecpids

Shared Light

In the quiet corners of a dimly lit room, I ponder the flicker of a flame, the simple act of lighting a lamp for another. It seems so small, so trivial, yet in that moment, I am reminded that kindness is a shared glow, a warmth that transcends the shadows we carry. When I extend my hand to light another's path, I am not merely illuminating their way; I am casting light upon my own.

Each spark ignites a thread of connection, weaving us together in this vast tapestry of existence. I think of the countless times I've stumbled, lost in the dark, and how the gentle glow of another's compassion has guided me home. It whispers to me that in giving, I too am gifted. The light I share doesn't diminish; it multiplies, reflecting back into my heart, filling the empty spaces with hope and clarity.

Imagine a world where every act of kindness is a lamp lit in the night, where we all become beacons for one another. We are not solitary travelers; we are companions on this winding road, each of us carrying our own flickering flame. When I light a lamp for you, I am saying, "You are not alone." And in that simple gesture, I find my own path illuminated, the shadows retreating, revealing the beauty that lies ahead.

So, I choose to light lamps, to scatter warmth and light like seeds upon the soil. I choose to brighten the corners of another's journey, knowing that in doing so, I cultivate my own garden of light. For in this shared luminosity, we discover that the more we give, the more we receive, and the world becomes a little less dark, a little more radiant, one small flame at a time.

https://app.videogen.io/view/qjojze

Inner Battles

In the quiet corners of my mind, shadows gather, whispering secrets I never wanted to hear, truths I never asked to face. They creep in, uninvited, like a chill that settles in the bones, wrapping around my heart, squeezing tighter with each passing moment. Your worst enemy cannot harm you as much as your own unguarded thoughts. It's a haunting refrain, echoing through the labyrinth of my psyche, a reminder that the fiercest battles are fought not in the open, but within the confines of my own consciousness.

I stand before a mirror, but it's not my reflection that stares back; it's a collage of insecurities, a tapestry woven from threads of doubt and fear. Each thought, a dagger, each memory, a bruise. I hear the voices—familiar, insidious—telling me I'm not enough, that I'll never be enough. They claw at my self-worth, tearing it apart piece by piece, until I'm left with nothing but a hollow shell, echoing their cruel taunts.

I wonder, who is the true enemy here? Is it the world outside, with its unyielding judgments and harsh criticisms, or is it the relentless critic that resides within, the one that knows my every flaw, my every mistake? The one that waits for the quiet moments to strike, to remind me of my failures, to paint my dreams in shades of despair.

I try to silence them, to drown them out with noise, with distractions, but they linger, like a persistent fog that refuses to lift. I realize now that the greatest prison is not built of bars or chains, but of thoughts left unguarded, of fears left unchecked. So I stand, trembling yet resolute, determined to reclaim my mind, to arm myself with kindness, to turn the tide against the fiercest foe I've ever known—myself.

https://app.videogen.io/view/ommktj

Whispers of Existence

In the stillness, where the world hushes, I find the whispers of existence, the soft murmurs of life that often go unheard. It's in the quiet moments, when the chaos recedes, that I can truly listen. The rustle of leaves, a gentle sigh of the wind, the distant laughter of children playing, their joy echoing like a heartbeat against the silence. The quieter I become, the more I hear—each sound a note in the symphony of being.

Thoughts, once a cacophony, now unravel like threads of silk, delicate and intricate. I hear the stories woven into the fabric of everyday life, the unspoken words that linger in the air, heavy with meaning. The pause between breaths, the weight of a glance, the tremor in a voice—these are the melodies of connection, the rhythms of understanding.

In the depths of silence, I discover the pulse of the earth, the thrum of life beneath my feet. I hear the heartbeat of the universe, a steady thud that reminds me I am part of something vast, something beautiful. The quieter I become, the more I can hear the truths that lie hidden beneath the surface, the fears and hopes that dance in the shadows.

I listen to the echo of my own thoughts, the quiet revelations that emerge when I stop drowning them out with noise. Each insight, a spark of light in the dark, illuminating the corners of my mind where doubt once resided.

And in this stillness, I find clarity, a profound understanding that in the quiet, I am not alone. I am surrounded by the symphony of life, a chorus of voices that rise and fall, each one a reminder that to listen is to connect, to be present, to truly live.

https://app.videogen.io/view/uzudcf

Embracing Impermanence

Even death is not to be feared by one who has lived wisely. What does it mean to live wisely? To embrace the fleeting moments, to dance with shadows, to savor the sweetness of laughter that spills from the heart like sunlight through autumn leaves. It is the quiet understanding that life is a tapestry woven with threads of joy and sorrow, each stitch a lesson, each color a memory. I have walked through the valleys of despair, felt the weight of loss pressing against my chest like a heavy stone, but in those moments of darkness, I found the flicker of light, the glimmer of hope that whispered, "This too shall pass."

I have learned that wisdom is not merely the accumulation of years, but the depth of experience, the richness of relationships, the courage to face the unknown. It is the gentle acceptance that every beginning must have an end, and that every breath is a gift, a fleeting miracle. I have watched the seasons change, the flowers bloom and wither, and I have marveled at the beauty of it all—the impermanence, the fragility, the exquisite dance of existence.

To fear death is to deny the very essence of life, to cling to the illusion of permanence in a world that thrives on change. I have loved fiercely, I have laughed until I cried, I have embraced the chaos and the calm, and in doing so, I have woven a life rich with meaning. So when the time comes, when the final curtain falls and the stage is empty, I will not tremble at the thought of departure. I will greet it with open arms, a heart full of gratitude, for I have lived, truly lived, and in that living, I have found my peace.

https://app.videogen.io/view/iyabwp

From The Philosophy Of Immanuel Kant

Pursuit of Happiness

The rules of happiness: Something to do, they say, and I ponder the weight of that phrase, the gravity of purpose. I find myself standing at the edge of a bustling city, where the rhythm of life pulses through the streets, and I am just a heartbeat among many. I could choose to chase after dreams, to paint with colors that only I can see, to write stories that whisper truths to the wind. The world offers a canvas, vast and untouched, waiting for the brush of my intentions. But what is it that truly ignites my spirit? Is it the act of creation, the thrill of movement, or the quiet moments of reflection? Perhaps it's all of it, woven together like threads of a tapestry, each strand a testament to the life I choose to lead. Someone to love, a phrase that wraps around my heart like a warm embrace. I think of the laughter shared over coffee, the silence that speaks volumes, the unspoken understanding that binds souls together. Love is a dance, a delicate balance of vulnerability and strength, a sanctuary where I can shed the layers of the world. It is in the small gestures, the late-night conversations, the way their eyes light up when they see me. Love is both a refuge and a challenge, a mirror reflecting my deepest fears and brightest hopes.

Something to hope for, the spark that ignites the soul. Hope is the light that pierces through the fog of uncertainty, the promise of tomorrow's dawn. It whispers that change is possible, that dreams can take flight, that even in the darkest moments, there is a glimmer of possibility. I cling to hope like a lifeline, knowing it fuels my journey, propelling me forward

into the unknown. In this delicate balance of doing, loving, and hoping,
I find my essence, my reason, my happiness.
https://app.videogen.io/view/vyfmpu

Crooked Beauty

Out of the crooked timber of humanity,
we carve our lives,
not with precision but with passion,
with the jagged edges of our flaws,
the splintered remnants of our choices,
and the knots of our histories.
We are not the straight lines of perfection,
but the spirals of our stories,
the curves of our laughter,
the bends of our tears,
the twisted paths of our dreams.
Every heart, a gnarled tree,
every soul, a mosaic of scars,
each one telling a tale of survival,
of love lost and found,
of battles fought in the silence of the night.
We are the architects of our own chaos,
building castles from the rubble of our mistakes,
finding beauty in the asymmetry,
the way the light dances through the cracks,
the way the shadows play upon the walls
of our imperfect lives.
In the crooked timber of humanity,
we discover our strength,
the resilience that comes from bending
without breaking,
the grace that emerges from the struggle,

the art that blooms in the cracks of our hearts.
We are not meant to be straight,
not meant to fit into the boxes
that society has crafted,
for we are wild,
we are free,
we are the untamed spirit of creation,
the vibrant hues of our existence
splashing against the canvas of the world.
In this crookedness,
we find our truth,
a truth that sings in the dissonance,
that dances in the imperfections,
that whispers softly,
reminding us that from these twisted roots,
the most beautiful of flowers can grow,
and from our crooked timber,
we can build a legacy,
a testament to the beauty of being human.
https://app.videogen.io/view/fzdert

From The Hindu Vedas

Universal Love

In the quiet corners of my heart, a flame flickers, a love so profound it spills over like a river, weaving through the tapestry of existence. I stand before the world, feeling the pulse of life in every creature, every whispering leaf, every flicker of a bird's wing. There is a thread that binds us, a shimmering connection that pulses with the rhythm of the universe. When I gaze into the eyes of another, I no longer see a stranger; I see reflections of my own soul, fragments of my being dancing in the light of their laughter, their pain, their joy.

I have become a lover of all, embracing the beauty in the mundane, the sacred in the simple. I breathe in the essence of the world, tasting the sweetness of a child's giggle, the wisdom in an elder's silence. Each moment is a brushstroke on the canvas of my heart, a vibrant splash of color that enriches my spirit. I flow with the stream of happiness, surrendering to its currents, allowing it to carry me to shores unknown, where every encounter is a treasure, every smile a gift.

In this vast expanse of life, I find myself intertwined with the struggles and triumphs of others. Their stories become my own, their dreams ignite the embers of my hope. I am a part and parcel of the Universal Joy, a note in the grand symphony of existence, resonating with the harmonies of love that echo in the hearts of all beings. The more I give, the more I receive, and in this dance of connection, I discover the profound truth: to love intensely is to live infinitely, to embrace the world is to embrace myself, and in this embrace, I am home.

https://app.videogen.io/view/zgjvvr

Celestial Love Song

Sing the song of celestial love, O singer! Let your voice rise like incense, curling into the vastness of the cosmos, where stars twinkle like the eyes of the divine, each one a whisper of grace, a promise of joy. In the silence of the night, when the world holds its breath, may the divine fountain of eternal grace and joy enter your soul, cascading through you like a river of light, washing away the shadows, illuminating the hidden corners of your heart.

May Brahma, the Divine One, with His infinite wisdom and boundless compassion, pluck the strings of your inner soul, each note resonating with the heartbeat of the universe, vibrating in harmony with the essence of existence. Feel His celestial fingers dance upon the strings, weaving melodies that echo through time, that transcend the mundane, that awaken the slumbering spirit within you.

In that sacred moment, when the music swells and the air shimmers with possibility, you become a vessel, a conduit of pure love, channeling the energy of creation itself. The barriers of self dissolve, and you are one with the cosmos, a single note in the grand symphony of life.

Let the song rise, let it swell, let it pierce the veil of the ordinary, for in that song lies the truth of your being, the essence of your soul. Each lyric a prayer, each chorus a celebration, a reminder of the divine spark that ignites your spirit.

So sing, O singer! Sing until your voice echoes through the heavens, until the stars align in your honor, until the very fabric of reality vibrates with the love that flows from the heart of Brahma, a love that knows no bounds, a love that is eternal.

https://app.videogen.io/view/mtiwkp[1]

---

1. https://app.videogen.io/view/mtiwkp

Lotus of Stillness

Meditating on the lotus of your heart,
I find myself submerged in the depths of stillness,
where silence speaks louder than the cacophony of existence.
In the center blooms the untainted,
a radiant core untouched by the dust of the world,
where the echoes of sorrow dissolve like mist in the dawn.
Here lies the exquisitely pure,
a clarity that transcends the mundane,
where joy is not a fleeting moment but an eternal embrace,
and sorrow, a distant whisper,
fading into the background of a vast, unending expanse.
In this sacred space,
I confront the inconceivable,
the vastness that cradles all that is and all that will ever be.
The unmanifest, a gentle reminder
that everything I perceive is but a reflection,
a dance of shadows on the walls of my mind,
while the essence remains,
a formless presence,
a pulse of creation,
infinite in its forms,
each a fragment of the divine tapestry.
Blissful, tranquil, immortal,
the womb of Brahma,
where worlds are conceived and dreams take flight.
Here, I am reminded of the interconnectedness,
the threads that weave through the fabric of being,
binding us all in a cosmic embrace,
where every heartbeat is a prayer,
every breath a celebration of existence.
In this stillness,

I shed the weight of my worries,
the burdens of yesterday,
and I float,
a lotus unfurling in the sun,
radiating love,
transcending time,
anchored in the purity of the heart,
where the universe whispers its secrets,
and I am both everything and nothing,
a reflection of the divine,
in the sacred silence of my soul.
https://app.videogen.io/view/wxmswq

From The Writings Of Pablo Neruda

Timeless Love

I love you without the clutter of time, without the ticking clock that insists on measuring moments, as if love could ever be contained in seconds or minutes. I love you in the silence that stretches between our breaths, where the world fades, and it's just us, two souls entwined in a dance that requires no music. I love you in the simplicity of being, where words dissolve into the air, leaving only the warmth of your presence, a soft glow that wraps around me like a whisper.

I love you without the weight of expectations, without the burdens of pride that often taint the purest of feelings. It's a love that flows freely, unencumbered by the 'shoulds' and 'oughts' that society imposes. I love you because I do not know how to love in any other way, a love that is not a transaction or a negotiation but a gift given without condition.

So intimate is this connection that your hand resting on my chest feels like an extension of my own being, a gentle reminder that we are one, a single heartbeat echoing in the vastness of existence. When I close my eyes, it is as if your gaze lingers, a soft caress that lulls me into dreams where we are infinite, where our spirits intertwine in the tapestry of the universe.

I love you in the quiet moments, in the spaces where words are unnecessary, where the language of our hearts speaks louder than any declaration. I love you simply, effortlessly, because that is the only way I know how to love, a love that transcends the boundaries of self, where

there is no you and no me, only us, suspended in the beauty of this unremarkable, extraordinary truth.
https://app.videogen.io/view/pyhxki

Eternal Whispers

I love you as the night loves the stars, hidden yet eternal, a quiet rebellion against the brightness of day. In the hush of dusk, where shadows stretch and yawn, I find you, a whisper between the breaths of twilight. You are the secret sigh that escapes in the stillness, an echo that dances in the corners of my heart, where the light dares not tread.

I love you like the moon loves the ocean, a pull that is felt but never seen, a tide that rises and falls in the depths of longing. You are the silver glimmer on the water's edge, a reflection that flickers just out of reach, a promise wrapped in the soft embrace of darkness. In the quiet hours, when the world is asleep, I trace the contours of your essence, the way shadows intertwine with the fabric of the night, a tapestry woven from dreams and secrets.

I love you as the wind loves the trees, a gentle caress that rustles the leaves, a breath that stirs the silence. You are the unseen force that moves through me, a current that pulls and pushes, a tempest of emotion hidden beneath the calm surface. In the rustle of branches, I hear your name, a soft chant that reverberates in the marrow of my bones, a song sung only in the dark.

I love you as the soul loves the unspoken, the hidden depths that yearn to be explored, the places where light dares not intrude. You are the quiet understanding that blooms in the shadows, a bond forged in the silence, a love that thrives in the spaces between words, where the heart knows what the mind cannot say. In this secret garden of shadows, I hold you close, a treasure buried deep, safe from the harsh glare of the world outside.
https://app.videogen.io/view/pyhxki

From The Writings Of Plato

Hidden Battles

In the quiet corners of the world, beneath the weight of smiles, there are battles raging, unseen, unfathomable. Each person I pass, a warrior cloaked in the mundane, their armor crafted from the fabric of resilience. I see them, the barista pouring coffee with a flicker of fatigue behind her eyes, the man on the corner, his sign a testament to hope, the child in the park, laughter echoing, yet shadows lurking in the depths of their innocence.

What stories lie beneath their skin? What storms do they weather in silence? The girl with the chipped nail polish, her laughter a fragile shield against the chaos of her mind. The elderly man, hands trembling, clutching memories that slip through his fingers like sand. Each face, a mosaic of struggles, stitched together with threads of unspoken grief, joy, fear, and love.

I want to reach out, to cradle their burdens in my hands, to whisper that they are not alone, that the weight they carry is shared in this vast tapestry of humanity. But instead, I often forget, lost in my own battles, my own storms. I forget that kindness, that small act of grace, can pierce through the armor, can illuminate the shadows.

To be kind is to acknowledge the unseen, to recognize that beneath the surface, we are all fighting, bleeding, yearning. It is a reminder that every interaction is a chance to lift, to heal, to connect. So I take a breath, summon the courage to be gentle, to be understanding, to be present. For in this shared struggle, we find our humanity, our strength. And

in kindness, we can forge a light, a beacon for those who wander in darkness, reminding them that they are not alone in their fight.
https://app.videogen.io/view/kvlsww

Echoes of War

Only the dead have seen the end of war. What a haunting truth, a chilling echo that reverberates through the corridors of time. We march, we fight, we bleed, and for what? The glory of a fleeting moment? The hollow promises of peace that slip through our fingers like sand? The living wear their scars like medals, each one a story, a testament to survival, but the dead, they rest in silence, untouched by the chaos that once consumed them. They know the finality of surrender, the quiet that follows the storm, the stillness that envelops the battlefield when the last gun falls silent.

We are the restless, the seekers of meaning in the rubble, sifting through memories of lost friends, of laughter turned to screams. We cling to the idea that perhaps one day, we will find resolution, that the blood spilled will forge a path to understanding. But the truth is, war is a beast that feasts on the living, leaving us hollow, asking us to carry the weight of its legacy.

How many times have we sworn, as the smoke clears, that we would learn, that we would change? Yet here we are, time and again, trading compassion for conflict, empathy for enmity. The dead, they have seen the end, but we? We are the witnesses, the participants, trapped in an endless cycle of rage and sorrow, yearning for a peace that feels like a distant dream.

Only the dead have seen the end of war, and perhaps that is the cruelest irony of all. They lie in their eternal rest, while we, the living, grapple with the ghosts of our choices, forever haunted by the echoes of battles fought and lives lost, searching for a light that seems just out of reach.
https://app.videogen.io/view/iudznv

Wisdom in Ignorance

I am the wisest man alive,
for I know one thing,
and that is that I know nothing.
In the vast expanse of existence,
where stars flicker like distant thoughts,
I stand, a speck of dust in the universe,
a whisper in the cacophony of creation,
and I embrace my ignorance.
What is wisdom, after all?
Is it the accumulation of facts,
the memorization of dates and names,
the ability to regurgitate knowledge
like a parrot in a gilded cage?
No, wisdom is the acceptance of limits,
the recognition that the more I learn,
the more I realize how little I grasp.
I see the world through a fractured lens,
each shard reflecting a truth,
yet none capturing the whole.
I wander through the labyrinth of thought,
each turn revealing a new question,
each answer dissolving like mist in the morning sun.
I am a seeker, a traveler on this winding path,
with no destination, only the journey,
and in that journey, I find freedom.
To know nothing is to be open,
to be curious, to embrace the unknown.
It is to dance with uncertainty,
to laugh in the face of complexity,
to find beauty in the chaos of existence.
I am the wisest man alive,

not because I possess knowledge,
but because I revel in my unknowing.
I hold my ignorance like a lantern,
its flickering flame illuminating the shadows,
guiding me through the dark alleys of doubt.
And in this light, I find connection,
with every soul who dares to ask,
who dares to wonder,
who dares to admit,
that we are all, in our own ways,
the wisest fools alive.
https://app.videogen.io/view/kauxwg

The Measure of a Man

What is the measure of a man? Is it the weight of his words, the echo of his laughter, the shadows cast by his choices? Power, that elusive spark, a flame that can warm or consume, a tool or a weapon, depending on the hands that wield it. It's not the crown on his head or the title on his door, but the quiet moments when no one is watching, when the world is still, and the heart is laid bare.

A man can rise, can conquer, can stand atop the world, but what then? Does he stretch out his hand to lift others, or does he hoard the light, casting others into darkness? The measure is not in the heights he reaches but in the depths he understands. It's in the decisions made in the silence, when the roar of the crowd fades, and it's just him and his conscience, wrestling with the weight of his choices.

Power can be a river, flowing freely, nourishing the land, or it can be a dam, holding back the tide, a fortress for the few. It can elevate or it can destroy. A man's legacy is written not in the monuments he builds but in the lives he touches, the kindness he sows, the compassion that flows from his hands.

To wield power is to dance on a precipice, to balance ambition with humility, to know that every action ripples through the fabric of existence. The measure of a man is not in his triumphs but in his trials, in the moments of grace when he chooses to serve rather than to be served, to love rather than to fear. In the end, it's not the power itself that defines him, but what he does with it, how he shapes the world around him, how he becomes a beacon or a shadow, a force for good or a whisper of regret. https://app.videogen.io/view/jwkibh

From The Writings Of Socrates

The Seeds of Wonder

Wonder is the beginning of wisdom, they say, but what is wonder if not the spark that ignites the mind, a flicker of light in the vast darkness of ignorance? It is the child's gaze, wide and unfiltered, drinking in the world like a parched traveler in a desert oasis, each droplet of beauty a revelation. The first time you see the stars, a universe sprawling before you, each twinkle a story, a whisper from eons past. You stand there, breathless, caught in the web of possibility, and in that moment, you grasp the enormity of existence, the dance of atoms and galaxies, the pulse of life itself.

Wonder is the question that tumbles from your lips, unrefined and raw, why is the sky blue, why do leaves change, why do we love? It is the insatiable thirst for understanding that drives us to explore, to dig deeper, to peel back the layers of reality like the petals of a flower, each layer revealing more questions, more mysteries. With every answer, the horizon expands, and wisdom blooms like wildflowers in a forgotten meadow, vibrant and wild, untamed by the confines of certainty.

But wisdom is not the end; it is the journey, a winding path paved with curiosity and doubt, where every stumble is a lesson, every misstep a chance to grow. The wise know that to wonder is to embrace uncertainty, to dance with the unknown, to hold the questions close and allow them to shape you. It is the willingness to be vulnerable, to admit that we do not know, that we are but tiny specks in the grand tapestry of existence, yet still, we seek, we question, we wonder. And in that wonder, we find the seeds of wisdom, waiting patiently to take root in the fertile soil of our minds.

https://app.videogen.io/view/kasiua

The Depth of Existence

What is it to live, to breathe, to wake each day, eyes opening to the same ceiling, the same walls, the same routine, a clock ticking, hands moving, time slipping like water through fingers? The unexamined life, they say, is not worth living, but what does it mean to examine? To peel back the layers of existence, to question the why of every breath, every heartbeat, every moment that passes, like whispers lost in the wind?

I wander through the corridors of my mind, each thought a door, each memory a window, and outside, the world spins on, indifferent to my inner turmoil. I ask myself, what do I truly want? What dreams lie dormant, buried beneath the weight of obligation and expectation? I see faces, familiar yet distant, love tangled in the mundane, laughter echoing in the silence of unspoken truths.

What of passion? What of desire? I feel them flicker, like candle flames, yearning for air, for acknowledgment. But my hands are tied, my heart a cage, and I wonder, is this all there is? The grind of the everyday, the safety of the known, the comfort of routine, but at what cost?

To examine is to confront the shadows, to embrace the light, to dance with fear, to question the very fabric of reality. It is to dive deep into the ocean of self, to wrestle with the currents of doubt, to emerge, gasping, with clarity. The unexamined life, a hollow shell, echoes of laughter but no depth, no soul.

So I choose to ponder, to reflect, to seek the richness of existence, to savor the bittersweet, to live fully, to be alive, not just in body but in spirit. I will not let the days slip away like grains of sand, for in examination, I find meaning, purpose, a life worth living.

https://app.videogen.io/view/wlchvx

Inner Revolution

In the quiet corners of my mind, I hear the echo of a truth, a whisper that stirs the dust of complacency. Let him who would move the world first move himself. It dances on the edge of my consciousness, a call to arms, a gentle nudge toward the mirror. The world, vast and sprawling, teeming with dreams and despair, waits, breath held, for the first tremor of change. But where does it begin? Not in the clamor of grand gestures or the cacophony of revolution, but in the stillness of the heart.

I stand before that mirror, the reflection a mosaic of hopes and fears, a tapestry woven with threads of who I am and who I wish to be. The world outside rages, a tempest of voices demanding attention, yet the most profound revolution begins in silence, in the quiet resolve to shift the weight of my own existence. To move is to confront the inertia of my own life, to peel back the layers of habit that cling like ivy, suffocating the roots of my potential.

What does it mean to move? To take that first step, to shake off the dust of yesterday? It means embracing the discomfort, the uncertainty, the trembling of my own resolve. It means recognizing that change is not a distant star, but a flicker within, waiting for the spark of intention. It is the realization that the world is a reflection of my choices, my actions, my willingness to engage with the chaos.

So here I stand, poised on the precipice of possibility, ready to embrace the trembling energy of transformation. Let the world watch as I move, for in my movement, I invite others to join the dance, to awaken to their own power, to shift the tides of existence. The world is waiting, but first, I must move.

https://app.videogen.io/view/babyjj

Minds in Motion

In the quiet corners of thought, where the strong minds gather, ideas swirl like autumn leaves caught in a gentle breeze, vibrant, alive, each one a spark igniting the darkness of ignorance. They carve pathways through the fog, illuminating the vast landscapes of possibility, weaving tapestries of innovation and dreaming of worlds yet to be born. They speak of change, of revolutions in thought, of the way a single idea can ripple through time and space, altering destinies, reshaping the contours of existence itself.

Then, there are the average minds, those who dwell in the realm of events, recounting the mundane like a well-worn story, a parade of moments strung together, each one a fleeting shadow. They discuss the weather, the latest news, the happenings that flicker on screens, ephemeral and hollow, a carousel of the same tired tales. They find comfort in the familiar, in the rhythm of routine, yet they miss the pulse of deeper truths, the heartbeat of the universe that thrums beneath the surface of what is known.

And finally, the weak minds, those who gossip and whisper, their conversations laced with the poison of judgment, dissecting the lives of others as if they were mere characters in a play. They cling to the trivial, the scandalous, the petty, their words dripping with disdain, a reflection of their own insecurities. They build walls around themselves, fortresses of fear, never daring to venture beyond the confines of their small, narrow world.

In this dance of discourse, the strong soar high, the average linger in the middle, and the weak remain tethered to the ground, forever missing the sky. In the end, it is the ideas that will change the world, the events that will fade, and the people who will always be just that—people, lost in the noise of their own making.

https://app.videogen.io/view/cggzjb

Being and Doing

To be is to do, they say, a mantra echoing through the chambers of existence, reverberating against the walls of my mind, a call to action, a challenge wrapped in a riddle. What does it mean, this dance of being and doing? I wake each morning, the sun spilling through the cracks of my window, and I wonder, am I merely existing, or am I truly living? To do, to act, to leap into the abyss of possibility, to grasp the fleeting moments that slip through my fingers like sand, that is the pulse of life, isn't it?

Yet, in the doing, there lies a paradox, a tangled web of intention and consequence. I move, I create, I strive, but in the flurry of action, do I lose sight of the essence of being? I chase dreams like fireflies on a summer night, their glow ephemeral, their light a reminder that in the pursuit, I must not forget to breathe, to feel, to simply be.

To be is to embrace the quiet moments, the stillness that allows the heart to speak, the soul to whisper its truths. It is in the pauses, the reflections, where the essence of existence blooms, unfurling like petals under the sun. To do without being is to run a race with no finish line, a relentless pursuit that leaves the spirit weary, longing for the grounding of presence.

So I ponder, as I stand at the crossroads of being and doing, how to weave them together, to let my actions flow from the depths of my being, to let my essence shape my steps. To be is to do, yes, but to do must also be to be, a symphony of existence where each note resonates with the truth of who I am.

https://app.videogen.io/view/meyifo